STO✓

D1530218

YOU CAN'T SNEEZE WITH YOUR EYES OPEN

& Other Freaky Facts About the Human Body

YOU CAN'T SNEEZE WITH YOUR EYES OPEN

& Other Freaky Facts About the Human Body

by Barbara Seuling

LODESTAR BOOKS   E. P. DUTTON   NEW YORK

Library of Congress Cataloging in Publication Data

Seuling, Barbara.
    You can't sneeze with your eyes open & other freaky
facts about the human body.
    "Lodestar books."
    Includes index.
    Summary: Presents facts relating to human physiology.
    1. Human physiology—Juvenile literature.   2. Body,
Human—Juvenile literature.   [1. Human physiology—
Miscellanea.   2. Body, Human—Miscellanea.
3. Curiosities and wonders]   I. Title.
QP37.S49   1986   612   86-6304
ISBN 0-525-67185-4

Published in the United States by E. P. Dutton,
a division of NAL Penguin Inc.,
2 Park Avenue, New York, N.Y. 10016

Published simultaneously in Canada by
Fitzhenry & Whiteside Limited, Toronto

Editor: Virginia Buckley

Printed in the U.S.A.   W
10 9 8 7 6 5 4 3

Contents

1

The Amazing
Human Machine

☐ Midget General Tom Thumb, 3 feet 4 inches tall, a star of P. T. Barnum's circus, married teeny Lavinia Warren, 2 feet 8 inches tall, on February 10, 1863, and at their wedding cut a cake that weighed more than they did.

☐ The queen of France, Catherine de Médicis, would not have a woman in her court with a waistline larger than 13 inches.

☐ William Howard Taft, twenty-seventh president of the United States, weighed over 300 pounds. He once got stuck in the White House bathtub and had to be removed with the help of others.

☐ The tallest person ever recorded, 8-foot 11.1-inch Robert Wadlow, was already 5 feet 4 inches tall at the age of 5, and was still growing at the time of his death at the age of 22.

3

☐ People in the Canadian province of Quebec are approximately a size smaller than their fellow Canadians.

☐ In Borneo, children were considered old enough to go to school if they could reach an arm over their heads and touch the opposite ear.

☐ A law decreed by Benito Mussolini of Italy during World War II required a minimum height of 5 feet 3 inches for government employees. Former Prime Minister Amintore Fanfani clearly broke the law in 1954, taking office while standing at a mere 5 feet 1 inch, but President Sandro Pertini squeaked by legitimately—at a towering 5 feet 3 inches.

☐ When the architects of Lincoln Center in New York City studied human dimensions for the installation of theater seats, they discovered that the average American had grown considerably wider in the hips over the last fifty years.

☐ The human body can survive three minutes without oxygen, three days without water, and three weeks without food.

☐ Between now and old age, you will walk about 70,000 miles.

☐ Showing or extending an open hand in greeting, as in a handshake, goes back to our earliest history. It indicates that we come in peace, carrying no weapons.

☐ One out of every ten kids has probably had a sleepwalking experience.

☐ In space, astronauts had to learn what to do with their bodies in a state of total weightlessness when they went to sleep. Soviet cosmonaut Gherman S. Titov had to tie his arms down with his belt because once he awoke to the alarming sight of his arms floating in midair.

5

☐ Unless you are rather unusual, you will spend about one-third of your life asleep. If, for any reason, you are continually deprived of sleep, you will probably have hallucinations and eventually go mad.

☐ Salvador Dali, the artist, devised his own alarm clock. He put a tin plate on the floor, then sat in a chair holding a spoon out over the plate. As he relaxed and slipped into a doze, the spoon went clattering to the floor, landing in the plate. The noise woke him up, and Dali went back to work.

☐ A report from a major insurance company shows that baseball players live longer than other people and that, among ballplayers, third basemen have the longest lives, and shortstops the shortest.

☐ Even bloodhounds and police dogs can't tell some identical twins apart.

☐ A jogger's feet hit the ground about two thousand times in one mile. When you walk, your feet hit the ground about one thousand times in a mile.

☐ Tom Dempsey, born in 1947 with only half a foot, was encouraged by his father as he grew up to play sports and take part in all activities like the other kids. He did, and even excelled at them. He holds the NFL's record for the longest field goal—63 yards.

☐ According to the prices listed in the catalog of a biochemical company, the ingredients that make up a 100-pound human being would be worth $3,563,590.70.

☐ Although you can't just go to a human spare-parts store and buy a new part, the age of transplants has made it possible to estimate, approximately, the cost of replacement. The following is an example:

lung	$100,000
heart	100,000
leg	2,000
elbow	1,200
toe joint	99
wrist	290
ankle	700
kidney	30,000

☐ Grover Cleveland, twenty-second and twenty-fourth president of the United States, had an artificial jaw. The operation, done aboard a yacht in the Potomac, was kept a secret from the public for twenty-five years.

☐ Wigmakers pay about $15 an ounce for human hair. Cosmetic companies buy fingernails over half an inch long for $5 to $10 each.

☐ Scientists are working on the principle of suspended animation so that astronauts of the future can sleep through long space flights without aging, using very little food and oxygen. Short hops might include one to Uranus (16 years) or Neptune (30.7 years).

☐ A microchip may soon replace a part of the body that is no longer working. For example, an implanted chip controlled by a transistor or computer could restore sight to a blind person.

☐ We are not the first civilization to consider disability income. Laws going back to the first Anglo-Danish king of Kent, Aethelbert, in A.D. 616, compensated a man for the loss of his fingers or thumb.

☐ Scientists believe that human beings of the future will have fewer teeth, no hair, and no little toes.

2

A Sound Foundation

☐ Your skeleton does not hold up your body; it is the muscles and ligaments, not the bones, that hold your body upright.

☐ A baby has a lot more bones than its father or mother. Pop, for example, has only one bone in his head—the skull —but Junior has twenty-nine separate bones.

☐ The hardest thing in the human body is tooth enamel.

9

☐ American foot sizes get larger with each generation.

☐ Your teeth started growing six months before you were born.

☐ Not all toes are created equal—your big toe has only two bones, while the rest have three.

☐ The only bone that does not connect with any other in the body is the hyoid bone, which is in your throat and supports your tongue and its muscles.

☐ The standard measurements we use are based on the width of a man's thumb—the inch, the length of a king's foot—the foot, and the distance between a man's nose and the tip of his thumb when his arm is outstretched—the yard.

☐ The distance between the inside of your elbow and your wrist is approximately the same as the length of your foot.

☐ The first Olympic stadium in Greece was based on the size of Hercules' foot. Six hundred of these, at approximately 12½ inches each, or a total of 625 feet, established the length of the stadium.

☐ When a man bends at the waist to pick up 100 pounds, about three-quarters of a ton of force is exerted on the disc between his last vertebra and his pelvis.

☐ By the end of the day, a person has shrunk about an inch—temporarily. The next morning, he's back to his old height again.

☐ A karate expert can break a board with his bare hand because the bones of the hand compress in the collision. Bones can withstand greater compression than wood.

☐ When they were looking for a way to protect the heads of football players, researchers studied the woodpecker because this bird hammers steadily with its head without suffering injury. A helmet was designed with air spaces similar to those in the woodpecker's skull, which act as shock absorbers.

☐ Bone is very light, and full of tiny holes. Your skeleton accounts for only 14 percent of your total body weight.

☐ Some cavalrymen rode their horses so rigorously that they grew additional bone in their backsides and thighs. The added stress of prolonged physical activity causes the bone to grow heavier and stronger. On the other hand, lack of physical activity results in bone loss. Astronauts, after long space voyages, show a remarkable loss of bone.

☐ Your bone cells replace themselves in a rapid exchange, resulting in a brand-new skeleton about every two years.

☐ Modern research indicates that, in the future, electrical current may be used to regenerate bone growth. In other words, if a person loses an arm, he may be able to grow another.

☐ A prisoner in a German jail, serving a six-year sentence for robbery, used his teeth to escape. He gnawed away at the wooden bars of his cell until he could squeeze out. Alas, although he chewed his way to freedom, he was caught and put in jail again—this time behind iron bars.

☐ Teeth have been transplanted, but they fall out after a few years.

☐ There was no junk food in Herculaneum, the ancient Roman city that was buried in hot lava in A.D. 79 after Mount Vesuvius erupted. According to experts who studied the skeletons of the victims, most skeletons—including those of two octogenarians—had all their teeth.

☐ Some people were afraid of the first X rays because they believed their bodies could be seen right through their clothes.

3

Outer Coverings

☐ If you had no skin, your body would dry up like a prune.

☐ Your skin weighs almost twice as much as your brain.

☐ A scab is really clotted blood that forms a kind of net over a cut. This mass of dried blood cells protects you while new skin is being made. When the new skin is ready, the scab drops off.

16

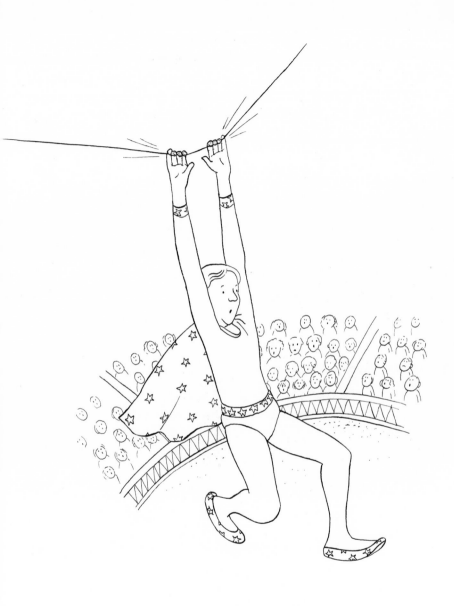

☐ The ridges in your fingerprints help you to hold on to things.

for Heather,
who has the gift of laughter

☐ No two sets of fingerprints are alike; even identical twins have different fingerprints.

☐ Chinese businessmen in the third century B.C. used fingerprints as personal seals.

☐ A 3-month-old fetus already has a distinctive set of fingerprints.

☐ Some of the best-preserved mummies in history, found in bogs in Denmark, were about 2,000 years old and so well preserved that local police were able to take the mummies' fingerprints.

☐ The skin of a woman, laid out flat, would cover about 17 square feet. A pregnant woman's skin would cover 18½ feet.

☐ Billions of bits of skin flake off your body every day.

☐ During the time of witch trials in the Middle Ages, birthmarks were considered to be marks made by the devil —a sure sign of a witch.

☐ After the age of 20, a person stops getting new freckles.

☐ It takes two hundred thousand frowns to produce one wrinkle.

☐ If you never trimmed your fingernails, they would be more than 13 feet long by the time you were 80 years old.

☐ Your fingernails are made of the same substance as feathers, claws, beaks, quills, and horns.

☐ Fingernails have been transplanted successfully.

✗☐ A human hair can support a weight of 2.8 ounces. A rope made of one thousand hairs would support you and three friends. If it were made of two thousand hairs, it could support three full-grown men.

☐ Your hair grows a total of 1,000 inches a day. Each hair grows $\frac{1}{100}$ of an inch daily, and there are 100,000 hairs on your head.

☐ Your hair grows faster in the morning than at any other time of day.

☐ Hair is dead. Hair follicles, or roots, are alive, and they push dead cells up through the scalp. This dead stuff is what you comb, brush, braid, and cornrow.

☐ A man could grow about 9 yards of whiskers in his lifetime. Shaving them off would take him about 3,336 hours, or 139 days.

☐ When Peter the Great, czar of Russia, could not grow a beard, he outlawed beards throughout his kingdom.

☐ The longest beard ever measured and recorded was that of a Norwegian man, Hans Langseth, born in 1846, who emigrated to the United States. His beard was 17½ feet long when he died in 1927. It is now in the Smithsonian Institution in Washington, D.C.

☐ Goose bumps are the places where hairs used to be. In days when humans were a lot hairier, the body's response to cold was that the hairs stood on end. The hairs created a trap for air, which acted as an insulating blanket against the cold. Now, with humans growing less hairy, all that happens is the initial response of the body, and little bumps rise where hairs used to be.

Beneath the Surface

☐ A human being is 60 percent water. Losing one-tenth of that amount can be fatal. You can lose far more blood —more than 3 quarts—and live.

☐ A person living in a hot climate can sweat as much as 3 gallons a day.

☐ Studies show that since a person starts to feel better as soon as he starts crying, all tears are tears of joy.

□ Mountain man Jedediah Smith saved the lives of two members of a trapping party in South Dakota who had fainted from loss of water. He buried them in sand up to their necks to keep their bodies from drying out, then went to find a water hole, filled his canteen, and returned to revive the dying men.

☐ A human being in bare feet leaves such a strong scent in his footprints that it is possible for another person to follow his trail.

☐ Astronauts wear air-conditioned underwear. Their space suits get pretty warm, since they are designed to hold in body heat. So when the body needs cooling, cool water is piped through tubes in the underwear.

☐ You wash your eyes every time you blink. Your tears are antiseptic and kill germs.

☐ Spit is useful. Your teeth grind up what you eat and mix it with spit so that the food can slide down your throat easily.

☐ One of the earliest studies on the digestive system was made by a doctor who examined a living stomach through an open window caused by a gunshot. A youth stationed at Fort Mackinac, an army post occupied by U.S. troops after the War of 1812, shot himself by accident. The hole that was made in his stomach remained as he recovered, and his physician took the opportunity to study the inner workings of the stomach, looking in daily and making notes. The doctor later published a book on his findings.

☐ You cannot burp when you are lying on your back.

☐ The average person eats 3 pounds of food a day, or 1,095 pounds a year, or the equivalent of three whole elephants in a lifetime.

☐ Your lungs are lightweight enough to float on water.

☐ Your body is being renewed constantly. In one year, 98 percent of the atoms in your body will be replaced by other atoms.

☐ It takes thirteen muscles in your leg and twenty in your foot to turn your foot outward. You use seventy-two muscles just to speak one word.

☐ The workout that the average adult gives his muscles each day is equivalent to loading 24,000 pounds from the ground onto a four-foot-high shelf.

☐ Harry Houdini, probably the best escape artist the world has known, attributed his success to his well-trained muscles. By holding his breath for long periods, and by expanding and contracting his various muscles, there was no situation from which Houdini could not escape—including locks, handcuffs, chains, straitjackets, and sealed trunks under water.

☐ The average person expels about a pint of gas each day.

☐ Your small intestine is four to five times as long as you are.

☐ The average human being inhales 3,500 gallons of air a day.

☐ A runner in a 100-yard dash needs about 7 quarts of oxygen. There is only about 1 quart available in your blood, so fast breathing has to supply the rest.

☐ Aristotle, the ancient Greek philosopher and scientist, believed that the liver was the seat of the emotions.

☐ You can't sneeze with your eyes open.

☐ The highest recorded sneeze speed is more than 100 miles per hour—the speed of a cork shooting out of a champagne bottle.

☐ Your heart beats 72 times every minute. By the time you are 65 years old, your heart will have beaten about 2½ billion times.

☐ The left half of your heart is much stronger and better developed than the right half. That is because the left half has to pump blood through your entire body, while the right half only has to pump blood through the lungs.

☐ The Egyptians thought so highly of the heart that they did not remove it from a corpse, as they did the other internal organs, but mummified it along with the rest of the body.

☐ Although your heart weighs only about $\frac{1}{100}$ of your body weight, it uses $\frac{1}{20}$ of the blood supply that flows through your body.

☐ Your heart rests between beats. If you add up the length of time of these rests over a lifetime, you will find that your heart stands still for about twenty years.

☐ Certain people in India are able to control their own heartbeats. They can actually make their hearts stop for short periods of time.

☐ You cannot hear a heartbeat. The sound you hear when you listen to someone's heart is that of the valves of the heart closing. The beat itself is a silent contraction of the muscles.

☐ Inside your body, your blood is blue. It turns red only when it mixes with oxygen, which is what happens when you cut yourself and bleed.

☐ Every second, your body manufactures 2½ million new red blood cells. Within a month, all your red blood cells are replaced with new ones.

☐ A single blood cell makes about three thousand round trips through the circulatory system.

☐ Humans should rust, just like frying pans and bicycles, when iron and oxygen in the body meet. Fortunately, we have a neat built-in rustproofing system. Iron in the body is swallowed up by ferritin balls, which act as storage bins for waste iron until it is needed to make new red blood cells. Then it is released only a few atoms at a time, giving it no chance to rust.

☐ The iron in a human being could make one small nail.

☐ Zinc in the human body is an essential ingredient, but it can prove fatal if a person is bitten by a rattlesnake. Then the zinc interacts in the bloodstream with a protein in the rattlesnake venom, poisoning the victim.

☐ There is enough phosphorus in the human body to make two thousand match tips.

☐ The pressure of blood rushing through an artery has enough force to lift a column of blood 5 feet in the air.

☐ It takes about twenty-three seconds for blood to circulate through the entire body.

☐ The tiniest blood vessels, or capillaries, are fifty times thinner than the finest human hair.

☐ A person who is 25 pounds overweight has nearly 5,000 extra miles of blood vessels through which the heart must pump blood.

☐ Placed end to end, the blood vessels in a human being would stretch 70,000 miles, or almost three times around the equator.

☐ The knockout in the boxing ring happens when a boxer is struck a powerful blow that causes a chain reaction in his circulatory system. This ultimately causes the supply of blood in the heart, lungs, and brain to pool in the abdomen, and to decrease the circulation in the brain, resulting in a loss of consciousness.

☐ When we stand up, if we didn't have valves in our veins, all the blood in our bodies would pour down, filling up our legs and feet.

5

A Good Head
on Your Shoulders

☐ The human brain weighs about 3 pounds. If all the water was squeezed out of it, it would weigh around 10 ounces.

☐ In Siamese twins, one twin is generally right-handed and the other left-handed.

☐ It takes about $\frac{1}{50}$ of a second for a pain in your big toe to reach your brain.

☐ The only cells in the body that are not replaced are the brain cells. The supply you have now must last you the rest of your life.

☐ By the time you are 10 years old, one side of your brain is dominant. If your left brain is dominant, you will be right-handed. If the right side of your brain is dominant, you will be a lefty.

☐ The twentieth president of the United States, James A. Garfield, could write classical Greek with his left hand and classical Latin with his right—at the same time.

☐ Your brain, more complex than any computer, operates on about the same amount of power that would light a 10-watt bulb.

☐ In a glass display case in the Boys' and Girls' Room of the Omaha Public Library, there is a human scalp, attached to wavy blond hair with a reddish tint. The scalp was donated by William Thompson, a Union Pacific telegraph operator. On August 6, 1867, Thompson was ambushed by Cheyenne Indians, shot, and scalped. The sensation of the knife on his scalp woke him up, and he grabbed the scalp from the startled Indian and ran. The warrior did not follow him.

☐ Dr. Truman Stafford, a Harvard instructor at the age of 20, was asked to do an amazing feat of math in his head —to square an eighteen-digit number. The stress was so great for him as he struggled for the answer that he spun around the room, pulled his pants up over the top of his boots, bit his hand, and rolled his eyes before he answered —correctly.

The Kerr clan of Scotland, whose members were mostly left-handed, built their castles with outer staircases that spiraled up counterclockwise so that they could fend off swordsmen with a left-handed parry as they backed up the steps.

WHAT THE...?

☐ The highest frequency that adult humans can hear is about 20,000 cycles per second. Children can hear frequencies up to 40,000 cycles.

☐ The lowest frequency that humans can hear is 16 cycles per second. If we heard anything lower than that, we'd hear the sound of our muscles working.

☐ You get dizzy when you spin around because there is liquid in your inner ear that spins around with you. When you stop, the liquid keeps spinning, giving you a dizzy sensation.

☐ The first hearing aids, which improved hearing by about 20 decibels, were shaped like trumpets and held to the ear.

☐ Only one out of three people in the world has perfect 20–20 vision.

☐ On the inside corner of your eye is the remnant of a third eyelid. Some animals still have this protective lid, which closes from the center outward.

☐ Some identical twins are so alike that they can wear each other's contact lenses.

☐ You can't taste anything solid unless part of it can be dissolved in the saliva on your tongue.

☐ Each of the tiny little bumps on your tongue contains about 250 taste buds. Each taste bud can taste only one flavor—sweet, salty, sour, or bitter.

☐ The only letter sounds you can make without your tongue are *m, p, b, f,* and *v.*

☐ Your tongue is the most movable organ in your body. It can move in every direction because it has plenty of muscles and no bone.

☐ An ordinary nose can distinguish from four thousand to ten thousand different smells. The nose of an expert in the perfume business might develop enough sensitivity to distinguish thirty thousand different scents.

☐ According to some experts, noses are adapted to do a particular engineering job in their native regions. In hot, dry places like Egypt, long noses moisturize the air along lengthy passages. In humid climates like Kenya, where there is no need for extra moisture, there are short, flat noses. In cold places like Finland, long narrow noses warm the air on its way in.

6

Beginnings and Endings

☐ Every human being once spent about half an hour as a single cell.

☐ On January 8, 1910, a 9-year-old boy and an 8-year-old girl of Amoy, China, became the parents of a normal baby boy. They were the youngest set of parents ever known.

☐ The king of Siam had fathered 370 children by the time he died in 1910.

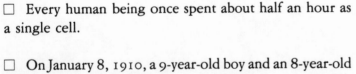

☐ The largest newborn infant of recent pound 4-ounce baby boy born in Turkey

☐ The smallest full-grown female human Earth, the Pygmy women of Africa, bear th in the human race, averaging more than birth.

☐ A woman in Russia bore sixty-nine there were sixteen pairs of twins, seven set four sets of quadruplets.

☐ Quadruplets occur once in every 512,0 tical quadruplets occur once in 16 millio

More babies are born in early spring than at any other time of year. September is the next most frequent time for births.

One out of every ninety births results in twins.

An Australian mother gave birth to twins so far apart that one was born in December 1952, and the other in February 1953.

In 1800, American women had an average of seven children.

The first incubator was a crude aquariumlike device developed by an unorthodox young Parisian obstetrician to save a patient's premature baby. Soon he was in demand for other cases, but it was very expensive to give such special care. To solve his financial problems and still save the babies, he put the infants on display at fairs, charging the eager crowds an admission price to watch them as they were fed, bathed, and diapered.

Two hundred years ago, nearly half of all women died before their thirty-fifth birthday.

About twenty-five hundred people in the Soviet Union are believed to be well into their hundreds. At the age of 168, Shirali Mislimov of Azerbaidzhan, USSR, was still walking half a mile a day and working a few hours in his garden. He said one of the tips for a long life was not getting married until he was 65.

The average life span of a caveman was eighteen years.

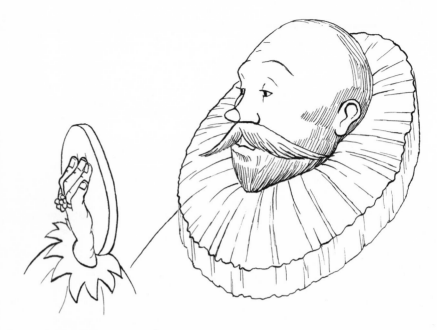

When Danish astronomer Tycho Brahe lost the tip of his nose in a duel, his vanity ruled, and he had it replaced with a gold one.

Czech composer Josef Myslivecek, of the eighteenth century, had no nose. It was removed by a doctor who told him the removal would cure him of a disease.

☐ Philosopher Jeremy Bentham ordered in his will that after he died his body be used for medical study and, when that was done, that the skeleton be reassembled on wires for anatomy lessons. Also in his will was a requirement that his head be mummified and stuck on top of the skeleton, and that the whole thing be presented at each meeting of Bentham's organization. To this day, Bentham's skeleton is rolled out at meetings of the Utilitarians—a group that proposes practical solutions for problems.

☐ Some scientists believe that humans have the potential to live around 150 years.

☐ The oldest American was said to be Charlie Smith, a former slave who was born in 1842 and died in 1979. At 65, Charlie Smith was starting a new job picking fruit in an orchard. When he was 136, his 73-year-old son came to visit him in a convalescent home.

☐ By the year 2000, one third of the population will be over the age of 60.

☐ In the late seventeenth century, a 152-year-old man was discovered living simply in the English countryside. He was brought to London and presented to the king, given employment in a noble household, and plied with plenty of food and drink. In a short time, he died—of an overly rich diet.

☐ Body snatching was a common practice in nineteenth-century Scotland. Medical students were always in need of new bodies to dissect to study anatomy, and the most likely place to get these was from newly dug graves. Relatives sometimes hired professional grave watchers to protect the graves of loved ones.

☐ Medical schools paid a flat fee for an adult's corpse and paid by the inch for a child's body.

☐ Mrs. Martin Van Butchell's will stated that her husband would inherit her fortune as long as he met certain conditions of her will, including a provision that she be kept aboveground. To get around these awkward terms, Butchell embalmed his wife, dressed her up, sat her in the parlor, and even had the public come in to view her as he enjoyed his new wealth.

☐ A rare modern-day mummy is the body of Lenin, former political leader of the Soviet Union, which has been preserved and put on display for the public since his death in 1924. The government will not give away the secret of how the body was preserved.

46

☐ The headhunting Jivaro of South America have a complex method of preserving and shrinking the heads of their enemies. No one knows for sure why these shrunken heads remain so well preserved, but it is believed that the Jivaro use a secret ingredient—the juice of a plant called *huito* in the process of boiling the head.

☐ So many people wanted to see the first cremation of a human body in America, in 1876, that a huge hall had to be rented for the service, seating fifteen hundred people.

7

Bugs in the System

☐ Laughing sickness, or kuru, a rare disease that affects only the Fore tribe of New Guinea, is 100 percent fatal. Until recently, the Fores were cannibals, and scientists believe that the virus for the disease may have been spread by eating brain tissue.

☐ Louis Pasteur, the famed scientist, carried a portable microscope with him, tucked under his coat, to see if the food served at friends' homes was safe to eat.

☐ Queen Elizabeth I stuffed her mouth with cloth when she appeared in public because her face had sunk in from the loss of her front teeth.

☐ In the eighteenth century, a noblewoman died from regularly painting her face with white lead.

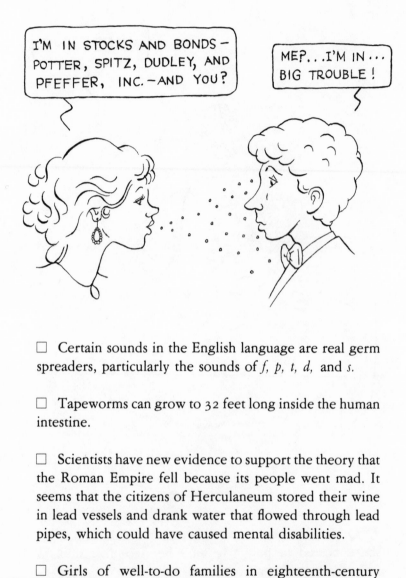

☐ Certain sounds in the English language are real germ spreaders, particularly the sounds of *f, p, t, d,* and *s.*

☐ Tapeworms can grow to 32 feet long inside the human intestine.

☐ Scientists have new evidence to support the theory that the Roman Empire fell because its people went mad. It seems that the citizens of Herculaneum stored their wine in lead vessels and drank water that flowed through lead pipes, which could have caused mental disabilities.

☐ Girls of well-to-do families in eighteenth-century Europe often had greenish complexions. Experts say the eerie malady was the result of delicate foods, tight corsets, lack of ventilation, and little exercise.

☐ Stone Age human fossils show evidence that our early ancestors suffered some of the same complaints of the body as people today, such as rheumatoid arthritis.

☐ Soldiers have keeled over in a dead faint during inspection. It seems the tension of standing rigidly straight can be so great that not enough blood fills the heart, resulting in a lowering of blood pressure and a blackout.

☐ Statistics show that a person's health can be impaired following a major life change in his or her regular routine. The death of a close family member is rated 63 on a scale from 1 to 100. The beginning of school rates a 26, and even Christmas rates a 12.

death of a close family member	63
personal injury or illness	53
addition of a new family member	39
death of a close friend	36
beginning of school	26
a change in schools	20
Christmas	12

☐ Queen Victoria of England, later learned to be a carrier of the blood disease hemophilia, spread the disease through just about every royal house in Europe. This is because her children, inheritors of the disease, married into other royal families.

☐ In the Middle Ages, it was believed that leprosy could be spread through the breath as well as through physical contact. Lepers were required by law to stand downwind if they stopped to speak to anyone on a road.

☐ A few rare human beings are born with a visible tail. Everyone has a tailbone, but usually it is hidden beneath the surface.

☐ One taste of the death cup, the world's deadliest mushroom, is fatal. As soon as its poisons enter the bloodstream, there is nothing that can be done. The mushroom contains five deadly poisons known to man, one of which is a hundred times as strong as cyanide.

☐ A 90-year-old man in Iowa has been hiccuping since 1922, ten to forty times a minute, and is still at it as of this writing. There is no scientific explanation for this, but the man says the hiccups started when he tried to lift a 350-pound hog.

☐ The hiccups of a young man admitted to an English hospital in 1769 were heard half a mile away.

☐ A workman in New England, trying to remove an unexploded charge of dynamite, set off an explosion that sent an iron crowbar through his skull. The crowbar was removed, with no apparent harm done to the man, although, afterward, people who knew him said his gentle manner was gone and that he was prone to severe outbursts of bad temper.

☐ Moses stuttered. So did the philosopher Aristotle, the storyteller Aesop, and the orator Demosthenes. Demosthenes used to stand on the seashore with pebbles under his tongue and shout above the roar of the waves, claiming that this cured his stuttering.

☐ It is estimated that 35 million Americans snore while they sleep. Some experts believe that snoring began with the cavemen, who made terrifying noises in their sleep to frighten away savage beasts.

☐ The highest recorded decibel level for a human snore is 69, almost the level of a pneumatic drill. Winston Churchill reached 35 decibels.

Healings and Dealings

☐ There is proof that Stone Age people performed surgical operations, sawing off limbs with tools handmade of stone or bone. One skull, found in southwestern England, shows that the patient was operated on—and also that he died before recovering.

☐ In ancient Babylon, doctors exhibited their most desperately ill patients in the public square, hoping that anyone passing by who knew of a remedy would speak up.

☐ In colonial days, one of the cures for toothache was "brimstone and gunpowder compounded with butter" rubbed onto the gums.

☐ The Aztec Indians began eating arsenic regularly as children, to build up their immunity to the poison.

☐ The Turks of ancient Anatolia fed cooked bird tongues to children who were slow in learning to talk.

☐ In the eighteenth and nineteenth centuries, leeches, wormlike creatures that suck the blood, were used to treat the sick. Several leeches were applied to the affected part of a sick person's body—in a ring around the head, for example, to cure a headache. Leeches are still sometimes used by boxers, after a fight, to treat a black eye.

☐ The first medical specialists were found in ancient Egypt. A sick person sent a description of his ailment to a temple of health, and the priest there sent out a physician skilled in the treatment of that condition. Surgery was sometimes performed, including the removal of stones from the bladder, cataract operations, and amputations.

☐ Hippocrates (460–377 B.C.), the father of medicine, is said to have set fire to a library when he was young—so that nobody would know what he knew.

☐ Egyptians mixed a concoction of hippopotamus fat and moldy bread crumbs to use as a medicine—and it worked. Some say it was a forerunner of penicillin—which was developed from mold.

☐ The Chinese paid their doctors for keeping them well but stopped paying them if they became sick.

☐ One Roman physician cured headaches and gout with an electric fish.

☐ Powdered mummy was once an important ingredient in European medicine. When the supply of mummies dwindled, "new" mummies were made from recent corpses.

☐ In 1595, Queen Elizabeth I's royal physican prescribed a mixture of powdered "muck, amber, gold, pearl, and unicorn's horns" to relieve the British ambassador's constipation.

☐ In seventeenth-century England, the local barber was also the local surgeon. The same brass basin that caught lather during a shave was used to catch the blood spilling from patients.

☐ Before anesthesia was discovered, a surgeon established his reputation by the speed with which he could operate. Famous surgeon Robert Liston is said to have cut off his assistant's fingers in his hurry to get the job done.

☐ One folk remedy for hiccups is to cover your head with a wastebasket and have somebody beat on it. Another is to drink nine swallows of water from your grandfather's cup without taking a breath. Still another is to spit on a rock, then turn it over. Or you can wet a piece of red thread with your tongue, stick it to your forehead, and look at it.

☐ Sofie Herzog, a pioneer doctor in Texas, removed so many bullets from gun-fighting cowboys that she made a necklace of them, which she wore throughout her life. The necklace was buried with her.

☐ A surgeon's favorite hobby, sailing, helped him to cure one of his patients, who had a severe curve in her spine. The doctor implanted a device fashioned after the one that helped keep the sails trim on his boat. This gadget held the patient's muscles taut so that the spine straightened.

☐ Horseradish was used at one time to treat complaints ranging from scurvy to baldness.

☐ Whooping cough was once treated by putting a live frog in the patient's mouth.

☐ It has been established that having a pet can help lower the owner's blood pressure.

☐ In modern India there is a hospital that is said to treat digestive complaints with various types of crushed jewels, such as powdered emeralds for liver trouble.

☐ In one culture, where modesty prohibits the display of the body, doctors may make available small figurines of a naked body which allow the patient to point to the afflicted part without removing any clothing.

☐ Some people were afraid of the first vaccinations, which were derived from cows. They were afraid that their vaccinated children might behave like cows.

☐ A crude method of inoculation began in the seventeenth century with the Chinese, who discovered that they could build resistance to smallpox by pulverizing the scabs of a smallpox victim and inhaling it through the nostrils.

☐ A doctor may now ask a heart patient to swallow the stethoscope. There is one instrument that is only an inch long and, once inside the body, transmits the sounds of the patient's heart to a microphone for the doctor to hear.

☐ Pegleg Smith, a mountain man, was trapping beaver when an Indian bullet smashed his leg. He wrapped a buckskin tourniquet around his thigh and amputated the leg below with a hunting knife. He whittled a leg out of hickory wood for himself, which he later pulled off and used as a weapon when he got into brawls.

9

Beliefs and Curiosities

☐ In 1770, British Parliament declared a marriage would be null and void if a woman had used artificial devices to seduce a man into marriage. Artificial teeth, wigs, and even high-heeled shoes were considered fraudulent.

☐ On the Sandwich Islands, chiefs were once accompanied by servants carrying portable spittoons. It was believed that if they could capture some of their enemy's saliva they would be able to bewitch him.

☐ People once believed that the mucus which flows down your nose when you have a cold was the brain leaking.

63

☐ Bronze Age people used drugs for illness but not to repair the body. They were used mainly to chase away the evil spirits that inhabited the body, causing the ailment.

☐ Peter Stuyvesant, governor of colonial New York, lost his leg during a battle on a Caribbean island in 1644. The leg was amputated, given a Christian burial, and accorded full military honors. Meanwhile, the rest of Stuyvesant went on to live another twenty-eight years.

☐ The Empress Marie-Louise of France could fold her ears.

☐ Francesco A. Lentini, known as the three-legged wonder, was born with three fully developed legs. He could walk, run, jump, ride a bicycle, ride a horse, ice skate, drive his own car, and kick a soccer ball with all three legs. Lentini boasted that he was the only man who came equipped with his own chair, using the third and shortest leg as a stool.

☐ The British once believed that it would take a freckle-faced king to conquer the Welsh.

☐ Mayan Indians sharpened their teeth to points, drilled holes in them, and stuck them full of jewels.

☐ Queen Elizabeth I set a new style when she took a bath every month, and others soon followed the practice.

☐ In eighteenth-century Scotland, citizens sometimes gathered at an execution to collect the criminal's blood, which was believed to cure various diseases.

☐ Frederick the Great of Prussia hated water and almost never washed his hands or face. Instead, he painted his cheeks each morning with red paint to look fresh and healthy.

☐ Soap, invented by the Phoenicians in A.D. 600, was not adopted by Europeans for cleaning the body until the Middle Ages. Before that, it was used only for laundering clothes.

☐ Anne Boleyn, second wife of Henry VIII, had an extra finger on her left hand.

☐ It is believed in some primitive cultures that a person's spirit enters and leaves the body through the mouth. Therefore, a well-meaning friend might try to keep the spirit from leaving by holding the dying person's mouth and nose closed.

☐ In the 1800s, people went to phrenologists to have the bumps on their heads read. Queen Victoria even sent her children to a phrenologist. The idea was that bumps indicated a particularly strong area of the brain indicating the person's special abilities.

☐ A person in Japan is more likely to ask your blood type than your astrological sign. Employers are even showing preference to certain employees because of their blood types.

☐ People once thought that a sneeze was a sign that death was near, so they started saying "God bless you" as a kind of condolence for what might be a last *achoo.*

☐ A Hindu fakir of Bengal, India, extended his right arm above his head in 1902 and kept it that way to show his contempt for, and mastery over, pain. He never took his arm down, even when a bird built its nest in the fakir's open palm. When he died, he was buried with his arm extended.

☐ On the frontier, there was a folk remedy for every complaint. To rid oneself of birthmarks, for example, it was necessary to rub them with the hand of a corpse or the head of a live eel three mornings in a row. A frontiersman in the northern forests would fasten the right eye of a wolf inside his right sleeve to ward off ills.

☐ Siamese twins Chang and Eng Bunker, who were born joined at the hip in 1811, grew up, married a pair of English sisters, fathered a total of twenty-two children, and died within two hours of each other in 1874.

☐ A farmer near Trier, West Germany, sells licks from his cow to bald people because some people believe that the cow's tongue stimulates the naked scalp, helping to make hair grow.

☐ In medieval times, if a man's eyebrows touched each other, that man was believed to be a werewolf.

☐ It was once believed that a vein ran from the third finger of the left hand to the heart, which is how the wedding ring came to be worn on that finger.

☐ Women in the Middle Ages used the poisonous juice of the belladonna plant to enlarge the pupils of their eyes, believing that would make them appear more beautiful.

☐ Frederic Chopin, the famous composer, was so afraid of being buried alive that he asked his friends to cut open his body before they buried him. His friends obliged, and Chopin's heart was sent to his native Poland.

Index

68

Bentham, Jeremy, 43
birthmarks, 19, 67
births, 40, 41, 42
blood, 16, 26, 30–32
  cells, 40
  pressure, 31, 51, 59
  type, 65
  vessels, 31
body scent, 25
body snatching, 46
body temperature, 25
Boleyn, Anne, 65
bones, 9–12
Borneo, 4
Brahe, Tycho, 39
brain, 33, 34, 63
breathing, 26
Bronze Age, 64
Bunker, Chang and Eng, 67
burping, 25
burying alive, 67

Canada, 4
cannibalism, 48
capillaries, 31
Catherine de Médicis, 1
cavalrymen, 12
cavemen, 42, 54
cells, 40
  blood, 16, 30
  brain, 34
Cheyenne Indians, 34
Chinese, 57
Chopin, Frederic, 67
Churchill, Winston, 54
circulatory system, 30, 31
Cleveland, Grover, 7
complexion, 50

consciousness, loss of, 32
contact lenses, 38
cremation, 47

Dali, Salvador, 6
death, 51, 52, 65
death cup, 52
deformities, 64, 65
dehydration, 24
Demosthenes, 52
Dempsey, Tom, 6
Denmark, 19
digestive complaints, 60
digestive system, 25
disability income, 8
disc, 11
diseases, 48–51, 64
dizziness, 37
drugs, 64

ears, 36–37, 64
Egyptians, 29, 57
elbow, 7, 11
Elizabeth I, Queen, 49, 58, 64
execution, 64
eyebrows, 67
eyelid, 38
eyes, 25, 37–38, 67

fainting, 32, 51
fakir, 66
Fanfani, Amintore, 4
feet, 6, 10, 11
ferritin, 30
fingernails, 7, 19, 20
fingerprints, 17, 19, 20

superstitions, 62, 63, 64, 65, 67
surgery, 55, 57, 58, 61
suspended animation, 7
sweat, 23

Taft, William Howard, 2
tailbone, 52
tapeworm, 50
taste, 38
tears, 23, 25
teeth, 8, 9, 10, 12, 15, 25, 49, 62, 64
Thompson, William, 34
thumb, 11
Titov, Gherman S., 5
toes, 7, 8, 11
Tom Thumb, General, 1
tongue, 11, 38
toothache, 56
tooth enamel, 9
transplants, 7, 12
Trier, West Germany, 67
triplets, 41
twins, 41, 42
  identical, 6, 19, 38
  Siamese, 33, 67

Uranus, 7

Utilitarians, 43

vaccination, 61
valves, 32
Van Butchell, Mrs. Martin, 46
veins, 32, 67
vertebra, 11
Victoria, Queen, 51, 65
vision, 37, 38

Wadlow, Robert, 3
waistline, 1
walking, 4, 6
Warren, Lavinia, 1
water, 4, 23, 24, 33
wedding ring, 67
weight, 2, 12
weightlessness, 5
werewolf, 67
whiskers, 20
whooping cough, 59
wigs, 7, 62
witch trials, 19
wrinkles, 19
wrist, 7, 11

X rays, 15

zinc, 31